WITHDRA...

...URCE C...TRE

D0227714

Robbers on the Road

to Sam

Robbers on the Road

Melvin Burgess

WESTERN ISLES
LIBRARIES
J30350114

A & C Black • London

TUDOR FLASHBACKS
Boy King • David Belbin
Robbers on the Road • Melvin Burgess
The Eyes of Doctor Dee • Maggie Pearson
Gunner's Boy • Ann Turnbull

First paperback edition 2003
First published in hardback 2002
by A & C Black Publishers Ltd
37 Soho Square, London, W1D 3QZ
www.acblack.com

Text copyright © 2002 Melvin Burgess

The right of Melvin Burgess to be identified as author of this work
has been asserted by him in accordance with the Copyright, Designs
and Patents Act 1988.

ISBN 0-7136-6106-2

A CIP catalogue record for this book is available
from the British Library.

All rights reserved. No part of this publication may be reproduced
in any form or by any means – graphic, electronic or mechanical,
including photocopying, recording, taping or information storage
and retrieval systems – without the prior permission in writing of
the publishers.

A & C Black uses paper produced with elemental, chlorine-free
pulp, harvested from managed sustainable forests.

Printed and bound in Great Britain by
Creative Print & Design (Wales), Ebbw Vale

Contents

Author's Note

You can get a better sense of the ordinary people in late Tudor times than for any other period right up to the reign of Victoria, because the playwrights then, people like William Shakespeare and Christopher Marlowe, were interested in real life. They showed us street life – the poor – as well as the rich, the rough and furious as well as the courtly.

One of the features of this time was the huge increase in people with no jobs and no homes. Begging was illegal – in theory – and the streets were full of people with no income – conmen, fake astrologers and alchemists, highway robbers, swindlers and thieves of all sorts – trying to trick or steal a living out of those who had. Then as now, it wasn't always the uneducated who ended up on the street. Some swindlers were highly successful men and women who pulled elaborate stunts to get their money, but most people with no trade survived from one day to the next, hunting for scraps.

The upright man who appears in this book was unusual in that he was licensed to beg. There were no pension schemes in those days, and it was common for noblemen to give their retired soldiers the right to beg for money on the road. Free money! It was a form of welfare, but the rulers never bothered to collect it in taxes off the workers before they handed it on. You only had to ask, but you didn't always get it, and you couldn't expect to get much if you did. Many of them had other, less legal ways of making money, but the cost of being caught was very high. I don't know who thought up the punishments they used at that time, but they were highly imaginative, often spectacularly cruel and many done in public as if torture was some sort of entertainment.

Meanwhile, everyday folk ran their businesses and got their children educated, just as we do today – just like the Biglow family in this story. School was hard. Beatings were a daily part of life and everyone accepted it. In the Lancashire town of Earby, where I used to live, the old Tudor Grammar School schoolhouse still stands – it's a Lead Mining Museum now. It's worth having a look at these buildings to see how seriously education was taken even back then. The coaching inn Will's father runs sounds like a lot more fun. The poorer sort of people would have got their beer at an alehouse, but a great amount of humanity would have passed through the doors of The White Lion as they went to and fro on the rutted, muddy roads of Elizabethan England.

Robbers on the Road is set in the 1580s. Tensions between Britain and Spain were high, political talk was all of spies and treachery and war. Religion was a big issue – we hadn't broken away from the Catholic faith for long, and you could be imprisoned or worse for following the wrong faith. This is what had happened to Francis's father and mother; his uncle Raymond would have been terrified that his headstrong nephew was going to go the same way and drag him and his household down on the way.

History is interesting, but the main thing is always the story. I hope you enjoy this one.

1 ✦ Will Biglow

My father says that as I have no brains and no cunning, it's just as well I'm so lucky. He's wrong about the cunning – I'm full of plans, me, things that nobody knows or could imagine. But the bit about no brains is true. My schoolmaster, Mr Japes, says that if I left my shoes off I might learn to count up to twenty, but he's only joking. I can count up as high as you like. It's the take-aways that get me confused.

I drive Mr Japes mad. He says my father is wasting his money sending me to school, but father says that I need to learn to count and read and write to make sure no one fiddles me when I grow up and have to take over our inn, The White Lion. I don't know about that. My father can't count well either, but mother counts like the wind! He says she counts so well, she can tell how much money you have in your pocket without even seeing it, by hearing it rattle and clink.

Mother's the clever one in our family, but my

father and I have all the cunning. If you're cunning, see, you can use other people's brains and don't need any yourself. See? That's why I always make sure I have clever friends, to save me the trouble of it myself.

That's Francis. Francis will be a great man one day, a general or an explorer. Oh, he'll be very, very rich. There! How's that for cunning? And foresight. When Francis is grown up and he's a great man, think of all the ways he'll be able to help me then. Cunning? I'm made of it, me.

Francis helped me right from the start. I started school late because my mother tried to save money by teaching me at home. She said that some of the things Mr Japes would teach me, like Latin and Greek, were of no use to an innkeeper's son, so why should she pay for me to learn them? But after a while she decided my skull was so thick that only a real teacher could do anything with me, so I went to school.

Because I was behind the others, Mr Japes put me in to sit with the little boys. Well, those boys were little, but they were cruel. They bullied me and hurt me every day. My mother said I shouldn't let them do it because I was so much bigger than they were, but it didn't help. They'd stick pins in me from behind when I wasn't looking and stamp on my toes so I'd let out a great roar of pain, and then Mr Japes would have me up in front of the class and whip me. Or one of them would let out a cry, and when Mr Japes asked what was wrong, they'd say I had hurt them, which was a lie – I never hurt a mouse if I can help it, unless it gets in and steals the horse-feed. And then, of course, I'd be whipped for that as well.

It was like this. I'd lost my boot in the schoolyard and one of the small boys was whipping my feet with a thin stick. He was shouting out for everyone to come and watch his dancing bear. It stung so much, he was making me hop round and round in circles yelling and hooting, and him and his friends were all laughing at me. In fact, the whole school was watching, laughing and shouting out advice to me.

'Take the stick off him!' 'Whack him one!' 'Give him a kick!' they yelled.

'I can't, I can't, he'll whip me harder!' I screamed and everyone was hooting with laughter because I was twice as big as him. But he scared me, with his long stick and his mean little face – I didn't know what to do.

'Call Mr Japes!' I was crying. 'Help me, before he whips my feet off!'

After a bit I began to see red. I see red sometimes, when people go too far, and then I get into big trouble because I hurt them too much. But this time Francis stepped in and took the stick away from the other boy.

'There,' he said to me. 'Now, why didn't you do that yourself?'

'He's too big and I'm too little,' I groaned, sitting on the ground and nursing my sore feet, and everyone laughed at me even more. But they were just being stupid. They knew I never meant it like that. Of course I knew I was bigger than that boy. I just meant that he *seemed* bigger, because he behaved big and I behaved small – that's all. But Francis took me at my word and decided to help me be big, so that I could protect myself from then on.

Francis got all the little boys and cut a notch in a tree over their heads, and then did the same for me, to show how much bigger than them I was. He made me lift huge stones that they could hardly budge – but it made no difference. They scared me more than I scared them, and that was all there was to it.

In the end, Francis decided I had to learn how to be scary myself, since I was so frightened. So he took me into a barn one day and spent the whole morning teaching me how to bellow like a bull or a lion, or some other fierce monster. It was hard work and hurt my throat, but by the end of the morning I had a roar so loud and fierce it would scare the pigs and make the timbers shake in the roof. After that, whenever one of the little boys came near me, I lowered my head and roared at them so loud that they ran away squealing like the pigs for their mummies. See – he's a good friend, is Francis. Teaching me how to roar was a clever idea. That's how I look after myself to this day. It never fails.

What can I tell you about Francis? Nothing, except that he's the most marvellous of us all. Everyone who sees him thinks so. He's a wonder of the world, is Francis. He's my best friend and my best luck all rolled up into one.

Francis lives with his uncle, Raymond Enterley. Mr Enterley's a rich man. He has servants. He even has a black slave. He makes his money from ships that sail all around the world and come back full of spices and silk and sugar and gold and everything that's precious. My father thinks Mr Enterley is a posing ninny. He's good at calling people names, my dad.

'That fat fish trying to wear trousers. That pee-pot with his dilly-dangler painted gold. That posturing pig with his silly beard and his manners that he learnt from someone else's wife.' That's what my father thinks of Raymond Enterley!

No one knew why Francis came to stay with Mr Enterley. Some people said that his parents were Catholics and had gone into hiding, or been arrested or executed. Other people said that his parents had had enough of him because of his bad ways, and they'd sent him away for a year in the hope that he'd be knocked into shape. Francis said that it was a secret thing, important business to do with spies and the Crown and Catholics and treasure from the Americas, and that we were never to say a thing about it to anyone.

Of course, you must be wondering what Francis was doing going to our little school. He should have had a private tutor, or a whole school of tutors, to teach him the things he needed to know. That was why he found it so hard doing what Mr Japes told him. It wasn't really his fault. Japes didn't even know as much as Francis did! Francis needed a squire or a knight or a lord to teach him the things he needed to know, not a common Mr Nothing like our old Japes.

Francis treated Japes very badly, but that wasn't his fault. It was the fault of his uncle. Mr Enterley's own sons, Francis's cousins, got a proper tutor who taught them at home. Francis should have been taught with them instead of having to put up with us lot – all craftsmen's sons and other common stuff, at an ordinary grammar school. It shows what a great boy Francis is, that he's prepared to get on with us, even though he's an aristocrat in all but name and we're just common folk. But it was a pity for Mr Japes!

He's a good man, Mr Japes, a good teacher. He's taught letters, Latin and respect to three-quarters of the town, and beaten every one of us on the way. In school he's a devil, you don't dare raise your head with Japes in the room, but he's a jolly man out of school. He likes his beer – he's often at our inn, cracking jokes and singing loudly. He loves singing, he sings in the church as well. The only thing that embarrasses him is women. When Bessie or Lottie try to chuck him under the chin or show him a bit of leg, he'll blush and bury his nose in his jar.

He used to be married but his wife died and then his son ran off to join the Duke's army. It nearly broke Mr Japes's heart, my father told me once.

'And poor old Japes has been as soft as butter on you children ever since.'

I was amazed to hear that. '*Soft?*' I said. 'Well, he nearly turned my backside inside out the day before!' But that's what my father said. He said the beatings Japes used to give the boys when he was a lad were so hard, it looked as if you had two creases in your bum after he'd done with you – the usual one going up and down and another one going from side to side – and that Mr Japes had lost the heart for it when his boy ran away from home.

Maybe. My father always makes out that everything was worse, or better, or bigger or smaller, or something more back when he was young. But maybe Mr Japes was younger and stronger then. By the time Francis came, Mr Japes had been teaching for a good forty years and his arm was too scrawny for a real good hit.

When Francis came to school that first day, he amazed us all straight away. He was dressed in bright colours and criss-cross stockings, and he walked around the playground with his hand on his hip as if he was there to meet the King. He told us tales of what had happened to his parents and why such a grand young man had come to our little school – I can't remember which story it was now, he has so many.

Not everyone liked Francis. A lot of the other boys were thinking, 'Oh-ho, wait until Japes gets his hands on this little scholar.' See, Japes has a way with new boys. He's kind to them but he's always very strict and if they step out of line – even a little bit – he whips them just to show them. Just so with Francis. Japes was kind and careful with him when he first came, but when Francis dropped his slate on the floor and told another boy to pick it up for him, Japes had him out at the front, made him bend over the chair and whipped him till the dust flew.

That was nothing unusual. No one took any notice. It was a usual sort of whipping – not too hard but enough to leave some good red stripes, so as to remind him over the week to be careful with Mr Japes. But then, the next day, in the middle of Mr Japes reading us out some Latin, what does your man Francis do, but start to whistle!

The whole class turned to look at him. Francis was leaning back in his chair with his hands behind his head, whistling a song.

'Can I help you, Mr Enterley?' asked Japes.

'Yes, Mr Japes, you can, sir. Those stripes you gave me yesterday are rather pale. I was hoping you could bring up a decent shade of red this time,' said Francis smartly. And up he went without another word and bent over the chair.

Well! What can you say? Of course, we all thought, Oh, he's going to learn better now. We thought he must have imagined that last beating was the best Japes could do. He must have thought that Mr Japes was as old and skinny as he looked. We knew better. That first whipping was just to say 'hello'. Now he was going to get the real thing.

Japes pulled out a good birch, twice as big as the little whip he'd used last time, and he beat Francis until he could hardly breathe. And it hurt all right! Francis was groaning and gasping and sobbing by the time he'd done.

Japes had to lean on his desk to get his breath back. I was sorry for him. He was an old man. Maybe he was too old for a teacher, because you need strength and spirit to keep us boys on our work.

'What have you to say to that, then, Enterley?' he panted.

Poor Francis could hardly speak, he was so busy just trying to breathe. But he got it out all right, so we could all hear it. 'Thank you, sir, and I'll be back for more next month,' said Francis. And he waited just a moment to see if he was going to get more before he made his way back to his chair.

Well! By God, what a way to carry on! Fierce! Tell me, now, isn't that the way a great man should carry on? Isn't that something?

'Japes ought to get a man in for the whippings,' said my father when I told him about it. He reckoned one of the grooms in our stables should do the job. But Japes was too proud to get help, and did his whippings himself. And they were enough, believe me, they were enough for any man in the country, unless he was Francis Enterley.

After school, Francis showed us all his stripes – there was blood. And he swore that he'd do the same next month.

'What for?' someone asked.

'To show him that he can't scare me,' said Francis.

All through the next month Francis was as sweet as a page-boy to Mr Japes, all proper and polite. But then, the next month, in the middle of Latin…

'Mr Japes, your buttons are coming off your pantaloons again. Can't you get yourself a wife to sew them back on?'

Japes swung round and turned yellow with rage. Even before he'd had time to find his breath back, Francis got calmly up from his place, went over and bent over the table.

'Let me have it, then, and try harder this time. You barely left a mark last time we crossed.'

And so it went on. Francis always behaved perfectly the rest of the time, but once a month, without warning, he'd suddenly come out with some piece of enormous cheek. They became pieces of legend, those insults! 'Mr Japes, there's a smell in here, have you farted, sir?' 'Mr Japes, do you think you could stand a little closer to the window? The smell is a little more than I can bear this morning.' 'Mr Japes, there's a snotter on this slate, is it yours?' Oh, it made us howl in the playground, but all the time we were all terrified.

Japes tried all sorts of tricks to get Francis to stop. He tried beating him earlier in the month, before he had time to get his remark out, but Francis just said it afterwards. He tried talking to Mr Enterley, but Mr Enterley just said that it was the schoolmaster's job to keep the peace in his own classroom. The rest of us divided into two camps – the Francis camp and the Japes camp. The Japes camp said that Francis was making the teacher look a fool and should have more respect. The Francis camp thought he was a hero, and that he did his work and behaved well. He was just pointing out that he was superior to Japes and never ought to be flogged by the likes of him.

I was in the Francis camp myself, but it was unfair to Japes, anyone could see that. He's a good man. When you leave school, he buys you a drink and invites you to sit down with him, saying he hopes that he'll have the pleasure of whipping your own children one day soon. And he does, too – anyone who can afford it sends their children to Japes. He doesn't hate children, he's just a teacher. The birch is just his tool. Like a carpenter has a saw and a ploughman a plough, a teacher has to have his birch. How else is he to keep us boys in check? But it goes to show that a birch is never enough on its own to teach a boy respect. Before Francis came, we all looked up to Japes and did as he asked us, but after that he never could keep the class quiet the way he used to.

2 ⊛ Francis Enterley

Oh, he's a great fool, a dunce, a clown, is Will Biglow – but he has a good heart. Will Bignose, they call him at school, because he has a snout like a cow – but not when I'm around. I won't let them say a word against him, or his family. I look after him. I've shared my lunch with him before now. I've fed him with my own hand and helped him, and he calls me his friend.

Which is taking it a bit far, of course. For one thing, he's a long way beneath me, even though my station is not what it should be, due to my enemies gaining the upper hand for a while – but that's a different story. For another, well, he's a good, loyal fellow, but, mercy, so dumb! You could tie a bell around his neck and leave him in a field with the other beasts and no one would know any better. If you found him eating acorns and rolling in the mud, you wouldn't be surprised. We are more like master and servant. Or faithful horse, perhaps. I've ridden him before now – he came to the gate at the back of my uncle's garden and carried me to school on his back for a while, until Japes put a stop to it.

Japes! Another great fool. The curse of my life. That bony skinflint of a man with his birch and his mean little ways. But he'll break his arm before he breaks my spirit, I can tell you that. It's among my greatest trials that I should be at the mercy of such a low-born lout, who mumbles his Latin through his teeth and can't speak French half as well as I can. It's an insult to my family. My father would thrash him for his insolence – but I have faith that God has put me here to prepare and test me for greater things. I swore to my father before he went away that I should be a loving and strong son, and love my God, my religion, my country and my family. I've done my best to keep my word until he comes back to collect me – even though my religion is against the law and my family treat me like a swine.

But when Father does come for me, there will be reckonings, I can tell you that. Japes for one thing, Uncle Raymond for another. The way he has behaved towards me is unbelievable. Of course, he was always jealous of my father, who was the eldest and had all the gifts of property and brains and everything else as well. To dress me in cast-offs, when his own brats have finished with them! To have his own children stay at home and eat bread and honey and learn their letters from a Frenchman, while I toil away with the peasants in this snot-hole of a school!

Of course, he tries to justify his common ways by sneering and saying that my father gave himself airs, and that a merchant can never be a lord, and that he got what he had coming to him for dabbling in politics. What does he know of great schemes and plots, and matters of state and honour? Uncle Raymond wouldn't know honour if it jumped up and punched him in the nose.

I remember the first time I came to him, after my father was arrested. I stood before him as my tutor had taught me, with my foot turned out and my arm held forward with my hat in my hand, and I bowed from the waist down.

'For God's sake, boy! What are you, a merchant's son or some mincing French fairy? Give me that!' He snatched the hat off me and flung it away. 'You'll do our kind no good at all like that. Get some straight-talking in you and stop walking like a peacock, before I kick you.'

You see? He's little better than a peasant himself,

for all his servants and cooks and fancy garden. And he's a liar, and he's a traitor. He'd do anything for money. Gold is all he's interested in. Hard to believe he bears any relation to my family at all. He has abandoned my father utterly. He pretends he's dead. My uncle's scared, you see. He called me into his study to tell me this 'news' of his. He was very sorry to say, but my father and mother had died in prison. He knew it was hard to bear, and he hoped that I would now be able to settle down and accept this as my new home.

'I think you must be mistaken, sir,' I said. There were tears pricking my eyes then, but I showed him no sign of it. I knew what he was up to. Like my father, I am of the Catholic religion. We live in dangerous times. My coward uncle was afraid he might be tarred with the same brush.

'Listen, Francis,' he told me. 'If the Queen says my backside is a pink turnip, then my backside is a pink turnip. If the Queen says that the Pope is a donkey, then the Pope is donkey. If the Queen tells us that God is a badger, then we'll be down the sett tomorrow on our knees to beg the badger's pardon. Do you understand me?'

'The Pope is greater than the Queen,' I told him.

'Then the Pope can look after himself. We are simple folk. We worship our God and fear our Queen.'

'But there is still truth, sir,' I told him.

'The truth is for God to show us when and if he sees fit. Now, if you want to remain in this house, you follow our ways and the ways of the country. You come along with the rest of us to church and keep your views to yourself, or you'll end up the same way as your mother and father, and maybe take the rest of us with you. Is that understood, Francis?'

So I had to agree, even though I had promised my father to be true to my religion.

Japes was the same. He took me aside and told me how sorry he was to hear about my father and mother, and that he hoped I could make a new life with them there in the town.

'I think you'll find my father and mother are not dead, sir,' I told him. 'Though if it pleases you to think they are, I won't disagree.'

He looked at me down his long nose and said, 'It does not please me. I am very sorry for it, very sorry indeed. I don't believe anyone should die because of God, and I am sure God would not wish it Himself.'

I was about to answer him, but I was unable to. I did not want to give him the pleasure of seeing me cry, though. I bit my lip and kept my face as still as I was able to make it, but I could not help my eyes from overflowing a little.

Japes put his hand on my shoulder. 'Your father was a brave man,' he said. 'But listen to me, Francis; the true Church is in your heart, and there you may worship how and whom you wish, and not all the kings and sheriffs of the world can stop you. Remember that.' He struck his scrawny breast and nodded at me. He had tears in his own eyes when he spoke. 'In the meantime, though, keep your lips sealed and don't mention the Pope or Queen Mary or anything Catholic, or you will bring disaster on to your own head.'

How dare he speak to me like that, in such a familiar way, and bring me to tears? What business was my family to him? What he did he know of the True Faith or of my father? Perhaps he thought that we would be friends after that, but the very next day I made it clear what I thought of him and his sympathy by asking him in Latin if he had peed on his shoes, or was it just dribble? He beat me for that as if his life was at stake, but it brought tears to his eyes as well as my own, and I was glad of it. That will teach him to repeat my uncle's lies, or to treat me like one of his little swineherds who has lost his favourite sow.

I think he learned to keep his distance after that.

So you see, I've fallen on hard times and have to mix with people who are not my equals. But I make the most of it! I gladly learn what poor little Japes has to teach me and only show him what I think of him once a month or so. I do as my uncle asks, although it pains me to accept charity, and I make friends with the common folk I have to mix with and try and look on it as a way of learning the ways of the world, which may be of use later on.

I intend to do great things. I would like to be an explorer, or a spy, or to go and take treasures from pirates and marry into some great family and be a part of the court. In the meantime, I have my schoolfellows to practise on. I used to have my cousins, too, but my uncle forbade it because he said I was filling their heads with nonsense.

So now I have Will Biglow.

Will makes a sort of servant for the clumsier jobs.

He does what I tell him and believes *anything* – anything! It amazes me how empty his head is. I set myself the task of filling it up with rubbish to see how far he will go, and there's no end to it. I once told him that one of his mother's chickens was a Frenchman in disguise, and he caught it and chopped off its head before it did any damage. Then he refused to eat it because he would never touch human flesh. Wonderful! He believes my father is a spy, you see, and that we are helping him gather information for the Queen. His father runs the coaching inn, The White Lion, on the edge of town, and I set Will to spying on the guests. The clot believes he is a spy for the Queen! Him – a lad with shovels for hands and a mouse-turd for a brain. I had to spend the best part of a week myself just teaching him how to shout!

You can imagine him trying to spy at the inn – creeping about like an enormous cow on its hind legs, trying to be quiet. I wish I could see that! And yet from time to time he does manage to get snippets of interesting information. I tell you, I have that whole family in the palm of my hand. If I wanted to, I could send them all to the stocks, or to gaol or even to the gallows. Of course, they are all on the make. Will's father, John, already spent a day in the stocks for watering down his beer and selling bread with chalk in it. Some boys threw turnips at him and knocked out two teeth, and the priest's mother came and emptied her chamber pot over his head, because he once accused her son of stealing his best pewter plates. It's a place for settling old scores, the stocks is. John Biglow's a villain all right – and only I know exactly how much of a dog he *really* is.

Most of the time the information Will brings me is nonsense, like how many sheep his father's buying or selling, or that the new beer is ready, or that a gentleman from Huddersfield is on his way through. But this time he was in a state of great excitement. He had overheard his father speaking secretly to an unknown man, hidden away around the back of the stables.

'It was all very secret and my father kept telling the man to keep his voice down so they wouldn't be heard. He was telling him about all the guests – who they were and how they looked, who they were travelling with and where they were going, and how much money and goods they had with 'em.' Poor Will beamed at me. 'See? So I reckon Father is a spy! And he was telling this gentleman stuff the Queen might need to know. I knew it, it's in the blood, us Biglows have probably been spying for ever! I wonder when Father will let me in on the secret so I can start doing it official for myself?'

'Yet my father once told me that your family is not involved in spying and never has been,' I told him. I know Will, there's no use pointing out common sense to him, it's beyond him. He's never seen my father, so he thinks of him as some sort of saint. It would never occur to Will to think that my father could be wrong.

He frowned and looked puzzled. 'Well, what can it be, then? And why should he be telling this stuff all in secret?'

Well, we found out soon enough – or at least I worked it out for myself.

You see, there was a robbery the next day. Yes, one of the guests at the inn was robbed on the road to Huddersfield – and he was one of the very guests Will's father had been discussing with this mysterious man the day before. The victim's name was Ben Callow, and he was travelling on foot back from the cloth market with a nice little bag of silver hidden away in a secret slit in his saddlebags. The thief went straight for the secret pocket, as if he knew exactly where it was and what was in it. And how did that thief know, you may ask? How else, but that John Biglow told him!

It's obvious! Everyone who travels that road passes by The White Lion. Most of them stop off there to water their horses, or hire new horses, or for a bed, or at least for a drink and a bite to eat. Many of them leave their valuables with the innkeeper while they sleep, for safekeeping, so Will says. And of course they talk to John Biglow as well – they tell him where they are going, what they have done, where they have been – and Mr Biglow passes the information on to a certain gentleman who makes his living on the road...

What do you think? You see what a spy I'm going to make – I have a gift for it! Of course, all Will did was run straight back to his father to tell him that the man he'd been talking about had been robbed. His father whipped him with his belt so hard, it shut even Will up – and he can take a whipping better than anyone except me. He was reluctant to do any spying for me for a while. It just proves that my theory is right. Helping a highwayman is not just an hour in the stocks – it's a hanging offence. I can tell you, it was a strange thing to think I had John Biglow's life in my hand. I could have gone to the sheriff anytime, but I never did. His son takes me for a friend. I'm no traitor.

But it did give me an excellent idea for getting my own back on Japes for all the beatings he'd given me. I swear I'll see that old man on his knees, begging me for his very life before this month is out – you just watch and see.

3 ♠ Will

It was the most wonderful plan you ever heard of – just like Francis! Boys were always playing tricks on Japes – getting him wet or covered in flour, or putting tacks on his chair, or getting him on the back with a snowball at the end of term – but this was in a different league altogether. This was monstrous. This was Francis!

Easter was coming and Japes was off on a journey – going to visit his niece in Huddersfield. He went to see her a couple of times a year if he could, because she was all the family he had since his son ran away, and she'd had a lot of bad luck in her life.

First she married a glove-maker who gave her four children, of whom two survived. Then the glove-maker died when a dog bit him and the bite turned bad. After that she married a brewer who gave her five children, of whom four survived. But the brewer was drunk all the time, and fell into a vat of ale and drowned. Then she married a carpenter who had time to give her only one child before he said that all those children drove him mad, and he ran away with a troupe of players and was never seen again. So she was left with a houseful of children and no means to support them. So, as often as he could, Japes would set out to visit her and bring a little money along, and try to educate her children as an act of kindness.

My father said it was because his own son had run away that Japes was so kind to his niece, but my mother said it was because he had a big heart and hated suffering (unless it was suffering that did some good, like thrashing a boy to make him learn).

But I'm telling too many stories and forgetting all about Francis's wonderful idea to trick Japes. You can tell when Francis has one of his ideas, because of the way his face moves and because a great light seems to come shining out of his eyes. In the schoolroom I often sit quietly watching him to see how all those ideas rushing through his head make his face move. I sometimes try to move my face the same way, hoping, you see, that ideas will begin to rush through my head as well. So far it hasn't worked – but I'm no quitter, and I keep on trying.

Anyhow, on this occasion, when Japes was telling us that we would be away from school a little longer than usual at Easter because he was going away, Francis turned straight round to look at me. I could tell at once that he had some great plan, because the light was practically shooting out of his ears and his nose, as well as his eyes. As soon as the lunch-hour came I ran over to him and begged him to tell me what it was. The idea was so wonderful that he made me run half-way to the moors and hide behind a wall before he'd tell me what was up.

'When Japes is on the road, Will,' he told me, 'you and I are going to give him such a fright, he's going to wet his pantaloons!'

I asked him how we were going to manage that.

'Will,' he said, 'we are going to turn highway robbers for a day and hold him up on the road!'

Well, I have to tell you, at first I was terrified! Some of the things they do to highway robbers if they catch them are just too much, even to think about.

There was a time a little while ago when Francis was teasing me very cruelly, because he claimed my father was in league with such a robber. Francis said my father was telling this man who it would be best to rob. I got very upset about it, actually, especially when Francis and some other boys started telling me of all the dreadful things that were likely to happen to my father.

Francis said that highwaymen got strung up by the necks and had their insides pulled out of a hole made in their bellies with a knife – all their intestines, yards and yards of them. He said that's what they'd do to my father if he got caught.

'And then, when they have all your guts out in a heap in front of you, they fling 'em on a fire and burn 'em!'

'No! You'd bleed to death while they were emptying you out,' said the other boy, John, whose father is a wine merchant.

'No! Because you have no blood in your guts. But you can *feel* everything,' said Francis.

Then John said they never did that – that was for traitors. He said what they did with highwaymen was, they hung them up in a cage on a chain high above the market place, where everyone could see them, and let them starve to death. 'My uncle saw one in York, once,' he said, 'and he was gnawing the iron of his bars with hunger and sticking out his tongue to try to catch the rain, he was so thirsty.'

'No!' said Francis, that was for Catholic priests (although I'm sure they burn them). What they did with highway robbers was, they cut off their right hands so they were only fit to beg, branded them with a red-hot iron across the face, beat them in public, and then left them in the stocks for people to spit at and throw dirt at and make fun of.

On and on they went. Can you imagine people saying such things were going to happen to your father? At last I couldn't bear it any longer. I just burst into tears and sat down in the grass by the road and cried my eyes out. Francis took pity on me then, but John ... well, John should have known better, he really should, because he'd known me for years and when I start to cry my temper isn't far behind. Francis told him to hush now, but John just kept on about a man he'd heard of who'd had the flesh pulled off his body with a pair of pincers that had been heated in a fire until they were red-hot, for cursing the Queen.

That's when I lost my temper. I jumped up and punched John so hard he went straight through the hedge we were standing next to and out the other side. Francis yelled out and ran round to the other side to have a look.

'Oh, my God, you've killed him,' howled Francis. 'Now, Will – what will we do? They're going to do all those horrible things to *you*!'

'No! I haven't … have I? Have I killed him?' I begged, looking desperately around me to see if anyone had seen me do it.

'Look how still he is!'

I began to cry again. 'Is it really true? Is it really true?' I blubbed, and Francis straightaway started thinking up clever plans for how to get rid of the body so no one would know … But before we could do anything more, John started groaning and woke up. I was so pleased I fell on him and kissed him, but John was furious. He was cursing me and shouting at me and scaring me. His face was going up like a pig's bladder, turning bright red and blue. Francis was trying to say it was all right, I hadn't meant it and that of course my father was a good man, and John was shouting that he *had* meant it, and that my father was absolutely a thief, and that he'd be hung up to die with his insides in a heap in front of him… And by then I was so exhausted, I began to cry again.

Well, things calmed down in the end. Francis made me and John shake hands and he explained how it was all just a big joke, and why should my father do such silly things when he had a good inn and such a strong son to help him? But it wasn't a very funny joke, and I think that Francis is not always as kind to me as he should be, when I am so loyal to him.

But now you see why he scared me when he said we were to become highwaymen. But it wasn't for real, you see. We were going to be play-acting! We would dress up in robes and cloaks, and borrow swords and daggers and whatever we could get, and see if we couldn't get Japes on his knees begging for his life. And then we would throw off our disguises and show him who we really were.

'But, Francis, won't Japes be angry with us for scaring him so badly?' I asked.

'No! He'll think we're so clever, he'll probably buy us both a drink,' Francis said. 'Japes likes a good joke. He forgave Jeremy Walker and Ambrose Price when they put frogs in his pocket last term, and he forgave John Wicks when he put a bucket of water over the door. He'll think it's the best and cleverest trick anyone ever played on him.'

'He'll still thrash us,' I said.

'Well, what if he does? We're used to thrashings, aren't we? And think, Will – it will be the most famous trick anyone ever played on a teacher. We'll go down in history. People will still be talking about it when we're a pair of old men!'

How about that? You see? I'd hardly known Francis for a year and already I was about to make history with him! Francis's brain works so quickly, it's like lightning. That very second he had it all worked out, from beginning to end. He had worked out that Japes would be hiring a horse from my father to take him on to Huddersfield, so I would be there to know exactly what time he would leave and what road he was going on. I'd even know which horse he was going to ride, if I kept my ears open. And Japes would be loaded up with money, since he always took some with him to give to his niece. All we had to do was to jump out at him, waving our swords and cursing like demons!

You should have heard Francis describing how Japes's jaw would drop, and how he'd fall off his horse into the mud and crawl about, begging us for his life! He had me creased up with laughter! And then afterwards, when he realised it was only us two, he'd pick himself up and thrash us, and then he'd shake our hands and tell us no hard feelings, and before long the three of us, me and Francis and Japes himself, would be rolling about, laughing at what an enormously fine trick we had pulled off! It was magnificent! It was pure gold. It had Francis's name written all over it.

4 ⊕ Francis

The plan was monstrously clever. The hard part was getting the Great Clot to understand what he had to do. The Great Clot – that's my private name for Will Biglow – thought all we had to do was jump out and scare Japes. But that was just the half of it. If we did that he'd know who we were at once. We had to be in disguise if he was going to be properly terrified. That was the beauty of the whole plan.

Will, of course, wanted to use his famous bellow to scare old Japes. I had to spend ages convincing him that it was no good. The bellow is something I taught him myself. Although he's as strong as an ox and nearly as big, Will's a terrible coward and gets scared so easily – even a babe in arms could bully him if it wanted to. Even teaching him to shout was difficult – he just couldn't understand about pushing his voice hard. In the end I did it like this. I stood a brick on end in front of him and told him that when he was shouting loud enough, he would blow the brick down. Since he always closes his eyes when he bellows very loudly, it was an easy matter to push the brick over when I judged that he was ready.

That bellow is actually a mighty monster. Will Biglow's neck is almost twice as wide as his head, so when he opens his mouth it's as big as the village duck pond. When he bellows, you can hear the bones in your head shaking if you stand too close. He can get the cows to stampede from two fields away. It would scare Japes even though he would know at once who was producing it – no one else in the world can shout as loudly as Will Biglow, so you see why Will wouldn't let go of the idea. In the end I agreed to let him use his shout when we revealed ourselves to Japes. When he was on his knees begging us to spare him, Will could open his mouth and bellow right into Japes's face. I thought, if the noise didn't kill the old man, the smell certainly would. Then we would pull down our masks.

Japes would be furious, of course. He'd thrash us both till the blood ran. With any luck he'd refuse to take me back to his ridiculous little grammar school. But I didn't care. Nothing would ever take away the pleasure of having the old fool on his knees before me, begging for his miserable, withered old life.

5 ⊛ Will

Every day after school for the rest of the month, Francis and I practised our act. That was how Francis looked at the whole thing – as an act, a little play. We have players come to the inn and put on a performance in the courtyard once or twice a year. It's always a grand occasion, like a holiday, with stalls selling sweets and little bites to eat, and so on. The players put up their stage and show us kings and queens and ancient history and the lives of the saints. Very often we'd be playing players for weeks afterwards. Of course, Francis was always brilliant, which, I suppose, was why he'd plotted our whole trick so well, with costumes and everything.

He'd thought the whole thing through, even down to our characters and how we would dress and what we would say. There was even a script! I was to run up from behind and growl near to Japes's ear to make him jump in the air and spin round. Then I would push him to the ground, grab him up to his feet again, shove him against a tree and say, 'Now, sir, what shall I take? Your life, your blood or your money?'

Oh, that was so good… that, 'Your life, your blood or your money,' bit. It rolled around the head so well. I spent ages getting it right. To make it even better, I had to put on a strange, growling accent, so he wouldn't recognise who I was. It was to sound like a wet cartwheel growling in its socket as it went over a stony wet puddle, said Francis. He made me say it over and over again, until I had it perfect.

Within a couple of days, Francis had got his hands on our disguises, too. I had a great, thick woollen shawl that hung down on either side of me, a woollen hat that hung over the side of my head – 'Like a great wart,' Francis said, and best of all, a pair of enormous leather gloves he'd found lying about in the stables at his uncle's house. They used to have a groom called Dickon, who was an enormous man – they must have been his. They were so huge, they made my hands look like two great spades. 'Just right for strangling,' said Francis. Then I had a long cotton rag to wrap around my neck and over my face. By the time I was done, I looked like the devil!

Francis had a black coat and leggings, and a woollen hood over his face that his uncle used for games of blind man's buff sometimes when his friends came round. But the very best thing was, he'd found himself a sword, which he polished till it gleamed. We had a bit of an argument over that sword. I thought I should have it, as I was the fierce highwayman. But Francis pointed out that I was to be the one close to Japes, and if he managed somehow to get his hands on it, then we'd both be at his mercy. He might even run one of us through with it if he was scared enough. So it was better to keep the sword back, in reserve, so as to stay out of danger.

You see, since I was so large, I was going to be the main highwayman. Francis was going to be what he called my 'shadowy accomplice', stealing behind me like a dark fiend. I asked him if he was sure about that, as it was his trick after all, but he said that if anything did go wrong, he'd be in a position to invent a cunning plan to free me, whereas if he was the one taken, whatever would become of us?

Francis explained to me that although I was to be ferocious, he was going to be even more terrible. He would lurk in the background, muttering terrible threats and angry oaths that would get worse and worse and worse, so that in the end, terrified of me though he would be, Japes would actually be grateful that it was me and not Francis he was dealing with. And if Japes did play up, I was to threaten him with handing him over to Francis. I was to say, 'Any more from you, sir, and I'll ask my friend to whittle your throat down to size!'

'I'll slice his liver out,' Francis was going to growl. 'I'll puncture his lungs. I'll chop his privates off and feed 'em to the crows!' That sort of thing.

He worked himself into such a rage that more than once I begged him for mercy during rehearsals.

'Don't be so soft, Will,' he told me. 'I'm acting!' But he had to come over and shake my hand and put his arm round me before I could go on – that was how good he was at playing.

He said that his aim was to make Japes wet himself with fear. I think he thought it would be good revenge for all the suffering he'd put on to us. But – I didn't very much like how fierce Francis got about it. I did wonder how much of it was acting and how much was his own true fury at how hard Japes used to whip him. I just wanted it all to be good fun for us all.

'Oh, it'll be good fun, Will,' Francis said. 'I shall certainly be enjoying myself, I promise you that.'

There had been no heavy rain for a couple of

weeks before Easter, which was good for travellers on the road. The roads turn into swamps when there's too much rain. The dry weather meant it would be busy at Easter, with people visiting relatives, or going to York to visit the cathedral, or on a pilgrimage. That was a good thing. Lots of people on the road meant lots of custom at our inn.

Our inn is such a wonderful place, the best place in the world – and one day, it will be all mine, if there's anything left of it. It's an old wooden building, two hundred years old, built in the days of Henry IV, and it really needs knocking down and starting again but we've no money to do that. The stables are even older. The big horses, Hero and Hester, could kick it down with one blow if they wanted to.

Hero and Hester are the finest horses in twenty miles. Even Raymond Enterley has nothing as fine as them. Rich men use them to cross the county as fast as the wind. There'll be a great clatter of hoofs in the courtyard and a gentleman will come galloping in on some other beast as big as they are, and wheel round and calm the creature down. Then he'll leap off and my father will take the reins himself, and the gentleman will jump down from the horse's back and walk into the inn. He'll eat a fowl and a plateful of mutton while my father prepares Hester or Hero, and then he'll jump straight back on our horse and gallop off again, on to the next inn. Sometimes I'm sent out to pick up our horse at The Bull or The Cross Keys, further down the road.

You can cross the whole county in a single day like that, getting a fresh horse at each inn on the way. My father does good business with it – but you need horses that a gentleman would be proud to ride. We have other horses as well – little mares for children and dainty ones for the ladies, and all sorts of mules and donkeys and nags for more common folk.

And there's my mother in the kitchen with the spits and the pots, and the scullion boys and the maids running about with fresh linen and straw, and the stable boys brushing the horses and mucking out ... Oh, it's a whole world, an inn. And one day I'll be the master of it. What do you think of that?

So, as I say, the weather was good coming up for Easter and my father was fattening up the chickens and sending out to buy wild fowl, and baking bread and cake, and brushing up the horses, ready for all the hungry folk who would be passing through. But then, three days before Japes was due to leave, what should come to visit us but a huge storm. The rain was rushing down around us all night. My father had men putting sandbags around the back of the inn, because the water flows in a stream right through the kitchen when there's too much rain. The wind was battering our poor old building this way and that, ripping planks of wood off it and banging the walls so the whole place was shaking. We were up all night calming down the horses – I really thought the stables were going to blow away altogether. But the morning came and we were still there, and so were they.

Our men were rushing about repairing things and finding the horses who had bolted, and that sort of thing. Francis and I were worried that Japes would put off his journey – but the next two days came clear and bright. The puddles grew smaller and the mud was not so deep. We still weren't sure – but I wheedled the information out of him. I'm good at that sort of thing, I am.

'Are you still going to Huddersfield to visit your niece, Mr Japes?' I asked him. 'I only asked,' I added, winking at Francis, 'so we know if we're to have a longer holiday or not. See?'

'Maybe the rain will have put off some folk and I'll get a better horse off your father, eh, Will? I'll want something that can plod through this mud,' replied Japes.

'Oh, you must go, Mr Japes – I'll ask my father to get you a good horse,' I told him.

He nodded and smiled, and I gave Francis another cunning wink, to show him how I had helped our plan along.

6 ⬥ Francis

I once told Will that Mr Japes lived under the schoolroom floorboards with the other beetles. Later that day I heard him ask Mr Japes if it didn't get lonely down there, and did he and the other beetles have much to dine on in the evenings when everyone had gone home? Perhaps it's the black coat Japes wears that made poor Will believe it. Japes thrashed him for that, and then he thrashed me as well for telling Will fibs.

What made it doubly amazing was that Will knows very well where Japes lives – in a row of cottages on the edge of town with Elizabeth Jinks and her husband, Robert, who makes harnesses and other horse tackle. On the morning of his journey to Huddersfield, Japes cut across High Barn field to get to the inn and pick up the horse Will's father was hiring out to him. My plan was to get him then, before he even got going. He'd be alone, not up on a horse, easier to get at, with the money for his niece in his pocket and not buried away in his saddlebags.

I told Will that after we'd done robbing Japes, we'd walk with him round to the inn and he'd buy us a drink to show there were no hard feelings – and he swallowed that as well, would you believe. Japes was not going to take kindly to being held up by two of his own pupils. My hope was that I'd be expelled, and if Will was expelled, too – well, what difference would that make? I'm as fond of Will as the next man, but education? – it's not really his strong point.

But there was one terrible flaw in my plan. Will Biglow.

Will's father decided to send a lad round to help Japes with his trunk across the field, and guess who that boy was? Will. He was only twelve years old, but he was already as big as an ox, and he could carry anything. His father must have fed him on beef and milk all day long to bring him to such an unnatural size. So how could Will rob Japes when he was carrying his things? It was a great shame. Despite the state of the roads there were many people preparing to set off that day. Japes would very probably be with a crowd. That meant hiding behind the trees and following him as he made his journey, and trying to spot a place ahead where we could hide and ambush him when he was on his own.

Of course, Will wanted to give up the whole plan as soon as we came to the first hitch. He whined that he had work to do at the inn that day for his father, and if he skipped off he'd not only get flogged by Japes, but by his father as well. He came running round to meet me before he picked up the truck and told me what had happened. I was still half asleep. It was half-past-five in the morning. On holiday I won't get up till midday if I can help it – but it was worth it to get my own back on Japes.

'Don't make me, Francis! We could follow him for miles and not get a chance, the roads'll be packed. I don't want to be flogged twice in one day.'

'No, Will.'

'But I'll be flogged,' he moaned.

'Don't be such a baby. It's our only chance,' I told him. He moaned and groaned and tried to get out of it, and I had to spend half an hour pulling faces to show him how Japes would look. Once I got him laughing, of course, he was mine. He forgot all about his father and having to work, and swore he'd follow me to the ends of the earth. If you can keep your men laughing, they'll stay on your side for ever.

I grabbed our costumes, and we sneaked round

together to Japes's cottage. Will knocked on the door while I hid myself behind a hedge. Japes was in a good mood. He opened the door, grinned and patted Will on the back, and said goodbye to Elizabeth. Then he stood outside the door breathing in big lungfuls of air while Will picked up the trunk. Off they went, Japes swinging his birch and saying how fresh the morning air was, and how good it was to be on the road, chatting away and singing snatches of song. I was creeping along behind the hedge out of sight, peering through the gaps in the hedge to make Will laugh.

It was busy at the inn. There was a man with a pair of mules going over to sell cloth in Skipton, an old woman and her son on an Easter pilgrimage to York, a couple of monks and other travellers. I hid myself away in one of the stables while Japes went inside to talk to the innkeeper and have some breakfast. When he came back out, Will was waiting there with the horse.

'Well, Will, here's a penny for your work. If you were as good at learning as you are at looking after horses, you'd be a genius!' said Japes.

Will took his penny and grinned and nodded his great pointy head.

'Nothing will fall off there – unless you get *robbed*!' he exclaimed in a loud voice, and stood up on tiptoes to peer round the horse and grin and wink at me like a madman. I was certain Japes would start wondering what was going on, but he didn't even glance at the stable where I was hidden.

'Well, heaven save me from that! But I'm not a rich man – not worth the robbing, really. There, you see, Will, poverty is the best protection from evil,' he said.

'Yes. Well!' And then you could see by Will's face that he had a great big idea. I was nervous. When Will Biglow has an idea, it's always a disaster.

'If you want to show them how poor you are, why not ride alone? Then they'd know how little you had to take!' said Will, and his whole face lit up like a beacon, he was so impressed by how clever he was. Why didn't he just shut up? He was going to give the whole game away!

But would you believe it? Japes actually seemed impressed by this stupid idea.

'As a matter of fact, Will,' he said, 'I prefer to travel on my own. I'll set off with the company, but once we get past Cutter's Ford I shall cut across the fields over to Marsden. It'll add a few miles to my journey, but I'll be able to call on a friend of mine there and have some lunch before I go on.'

Can you credit it? Japes was so dim that even a clot-brained nincompoop with a bladder for a brain like Will Biglow could make a fool of him! I prayed that Will would be too stupid to see how valuable this information was, but – just my luck – for once he spotted what was going on. He started clapping his hands together and whooping, and jumping up to see over the horse to try and make sure I'd seen how clever he was.

'Does my detour please you, Will?' asked Japes.

'Sir, it does!'

'And why's that? You're not planning on robbing me are you?'

Will stared at him and for a second I thought he was going to say, 'Yes.' You could see his face twisting and turning in an effort to think of something to say. Finally, with a great effort he opened his enormous mouth and bellowed, 'No!'

Japes flinched and wiped spittle from his face. 'That's a good thing, then,' he smiled. 'Perhaps you're happy that I'm going such a pretty way?'

'Yes, that's it, that's it, that's exactly right!' screamed Will, in a terror of being found out. And he looked over to where I was hiding and pretended to wipe his brow in relief that he'd got out of it. I was certain that he had given the whole thing away, but instead, Japes started going over his shortcut in great detail, how he would head across such and such a field and cut by such and such a coppice and under such and such a bridge. By the time he'd finished speaking, I already knew in my head exactly which way Japes was going, and exactly where Will and I would be waiting for him. It was perfect. The silly old fool was playing right into our hands!

A few minutes later Japes set off with the monks and the weaver. As soon as they were round the corner I grabbed Will and ran him out of the courtyard of the inn before his father or one of the grooms found a job for him. We ran as fast as we could towards the coppice Japes had mentioned, a little way out of Marsden. The track ran close to an old farmhouse that had burned down. A few of the stones from the wall were still standing. The coppice was ready to be cut, quite dense. We could be tucked away out of sight and yet be on top of him in a second – the perfect place for a highway robbery!

7 ☢ Will

Even Francis was impressed. Just as it looked like all our plans had fallen to pieces, I managed to wriggle out of Japes which way he was going. I got everything out of him – which track he was following, which fields and woods he was passing. How's that for cunning? Don't tell me I'm all muscle and no brains – you have to have brains like a sorcerer to do what I did with Japes that morning!

We rushed across the fields like a pair of carthorses. I wanted to overtake Japes on the way, and make clever remarks to him as we went past – about robbers, like I'd done in the courtyard – but Francis wouldn't have it. He said it'd be more of a surprise if Japes wasn't expecting us to be there, and he made us go round in a great loop. So we ran and ran and by the time we got there, we were both panting like dogs and trying to make no noise at the same time, in case he was already near.

The old place was just perfect for robbery. We hid ourselves down behind a wall amongst nettles and ivy and stumps of coppiced beech. We could crouch there out of sight and peer between the tall stems of wood to see whoever was coming along the path.

Japes was ages – he must have been going dead slow. We'd come twice his distance and on foot. He was so long, we thought he must be on to us – but suddenly we could hear the sound of someone singing – it was Japes, who else? He loves singing, he's always singing his head off. And then there he was, rolling along on top of his little horse without a care in the world.

'Oh, Francis – won't he laugh!' I giggled, hiding my mouth in my hands. I was sure I'd be laughing so much I wouldn't be able to do it.

'Shut up, you bonehead, he'll hear you! Be quiet!' hissed Francis – which I thought was a bit harsh, since we wouldn't be there if it wasn't for me.

Japes came closer and closer, singing a silly song, until he drew up right next to us.

'Grab him!' hissed Francis, and he pushed me forward so hard that I fell out of our thicket on to all fours. I looked up to see Japes's white face looking down at me with a little smile on his face – he must not have guessed what was afoot yet. Then Francis leapt out of the hedge with a sinister chuckle he'd been rehearsing for ages. It went something like, 'Ha, ha, ha … ho, ho!' and when he said that, 'ho, ho!', it would freeze the blood in your veins.

'Give him to me!' he yelled, and kicked me hard in the shin to make me get up and give chase.

I jumped up, lunged forward and grabbed Japes by the ankle, just as the pony decided it had some speed in its legs. It shot forward; I was pulling Japes one way, the pony was going the other. Japes clung hold of the reins and shouted to her to whoa up. He had huge long legs, Mr Japes, and he looked like he was going to split in half. But then Francis ran round the other side, slipped Japes's other foot out of the stirrup and shoved it up. Japes went over the horse with a yell and landed on top of me.

I was petrified that I'd hurt him, but he was already getting to his feet. Francis dashed around the horse and closed in on the other side, growling and grunting like a wild sow and swiping his sword in the air as if he was ready to slice Japes up.

'Mercy, sir!' cried Japes. And he started patting himself all over to see where he'd been stuck. It was gorgeous! I started to giggle, Japes looked so scared, soon but I soon stopped when Francis shot me one of his looks.

'Mercy? Never mind that! Let me at him, Barty, so I can slice his liver into strips for my dogs!'

That was my cue. I stepped forward, grabbed Japes by his quaking shirt front and growled at him...

'Now, sir, what shall I take? Your life, your blood or your money?'

Japes fell to his knees. 'Sir! My money! Take my money, I beg you!'

Francis held his sword by our teacher's neck and was staring down at him with a big grin all over his face. I was grinning, too, but I was feeling funny about it. It didn't feel right having the old man down on his knees like that. I was scared Francis would go too far. But Francis was enjoying himself. He began making sweeping cuts with his sword in the air around Japes's head to terrify him even further, but he terrified me as well! What if he made a mistake and cut him? Japes yelped in fear – then there was a noise behind us. I looked backwards and there was a huge, fierce man rushing towards us. His face was covered in a mask of cloth with holes for his eyes. I heard myself let out a funny little noise of surprise.

The man leaped forward and grabbed hold of

Francis by the neck, tore his sword out of his hand and flung him into the grass.

'You'd strike off his head, would you, you little cur?' he yelled. He picked up the sword and flung it away into the bushes. 'Drop your stick!' he told me, and I did what he said. I never saw a man look so deadly.

'Don't hurt me, please, it was just a joke!' I whimpered.

'Sorry!' said Francis, scrabbling to his feet. But the tall man just pushed him back to the ground.

'One more squeak out of you and I'll break you up,' he growled. And he stood there staring at us for a second, panting with rage. I thought he was going to kill the pair of us.

Mr Japes had got up on his feet again, and he came forward with his hand out to the man. 'Sir, you've saved my life,' he began, but the man shut him up.

'If I've saved it, then it's mine to give away again – hold your tongue!' he snapped. Then he turned his attention back to us. 'Two snotty little poachers,' he hissed. 'Two pesky young crows pecking at my meat. Two little snots waiting to be picked off.'

Francis cried out, 'It was only a joke, sir!'

I saw Mr Japes look curiously at him. He knew that voice. Francis had been using his special acting voice, but now he was talking as himself and Japes recognised his tone.

The fierce man saw what was going on. 'So, we all know each other, do we?' He nodded at Francis and smiled grimly. 'Well, then, let me introduce you better. Perhaps your poor victim will care to tell the sheriff just who it was that robbed him this morning? Let's see you. Take off your masks.'

We both took a step back and looked at each other. We'd not had a chance to tell Japes it was a joke! What if he thought it was real? My mind went back to all those dreadful things they do to highwaymen – pulling out your guts, hanging you up in a cage, burning you with hot irons. I didn't want to be tortured!

Francis shook his head violently, and began to speak very quickly and quietly in that special acting voice again. I didn't understand at first – it was only later he told me that he was trying to keep who he was hidden from Japes – although it was too late for that, if you ask me.

'This was just a joke, sir, but it is possible people will see it in the wrong light. I'm prepared to offer you a handsome reward – in gold or silver, sir, whatever you care – if you'll just give me time to go back home, I know my … guardians will be happy to make it worth your while.'

The highwayman just laughed at him. 'Well!' he said. 'It seems someone doesn't want to be seen. Are we all friends here? Well, then! Off with it – off with it now, or I'll prick your eyes till they burst!'

He stuck his dagger at Francis's face and growled – I mean, he really growled, it was a terrifying noise. I was certain he was going to slit Francis open...

'Take it off, boy!'

'Please don't,' said Francis, in a strange voice, but the man leaned forward and with one swift motion pulled the hood up over my friend's head. It was a shock to see him – he looked so white, and his eyes were so red with tears of fear.

The highwayman grinned. Then Japes started to speak and we all turned to him.

'Francis!' he cried. 'Oh, Francis! You'd even rob your poor old schoolmaster?'

'No, sir, no sir,' wept Francis, and the tears were pouring down his face. 'It was just a joke, sir, honestly sir … just to get you back for all those floggings.'

But Mr Japes shook his head. 'I don't believe it,

Francis. The way you were waving that sword around my head, I believe you intended to kill me. And now they will hang you – right at the beginning of your life!'

'No, sir!' begged Francis, and he flung himself to his knees and began weeping and begging wretchedly. I was ashamed to see him act like that. But there was worse. You'll never believe me, but he tried to make out that the whole affair had been my idea! I could hardly believe it myself. I always thought Francis was so brave and clever. You'd have thought he could talk his way out of anything, but here he was begging for his life and offering mine up in its place.

That's when my heart despaired. Until then I thought that Francis could hook us out of any trouble, but when I saw him beg for his life from that terrible, merciless highwayman, and try to blame me for everything, I knew that I was a lost soul.

'It was just a prank, sir, that Will thought up for a game and I was silly enough to believe,' he wept.

'Oh, do you believe that, Mr Japes? It sounds very convenient,' said the highwayman. 'And after they pulled you off your horse so roughly – a very painful joke that was, I bet! Ah, my robber sirs! I think you'd be better off running for your life. Do you know what they do with your kind? Mr Japes is just trying to make you feel better by saying that all you will suffer is a hanging. It'll be much worse than that!'

'But it was a joke,' cried Francis.

'Ha, ha, ha,' said the man, without cracking a smile. 'Now – let's see the other one.' He reached out to my face and plucked the mask away. I fell at once to my knees, my face streaming tears, unable even to speak.

'Will! *You?*' gasped Japes. 'Oh – and now they will hang you, too! How often I told you not to follow Francis, and now look – you'll be dead within a week!'

'No sir, please, sir!' I wept. But it was no good. Mr Japes was certain we had truly been trying to rob him. It was the end for us both.

8 ⚉ Francis

Everything was ruined! My whole life – gone! The world was at my feet one minute, and the next I was going to be hung up like carrion. One glance at that terrible man was enough to tell me that he had no mercy – he had barely even a soul inside him. I offered gold and jewels and begged for the love of God and life and love, and everything that was holy, but the filthy brute was without pity. He had come at just the worst time, when Japes was most scared. Our lives were in the hands of that miserable old scarecrow.

Just to make the whole thing worse, he robbed Japes of everything he had. He made him empty his pockets and then his saddlebags – he even made him take off his boots so he could check if he had things hidden in the toes. He took all the silver Japes had saved for his niece, over five pounds – how he saved so much out of his miserable wage I don't know. There were gifts of cotton and woollens and ironware and a leather wallet, and all sorts of other bits and pieces.

Then he put the whole lot back into the saddlebags, got up on the horse that Will's father had hired to Japes and rode off, leaving Will and me tied up, with Japes standing there looking grimly at us, just as if we were back in the school room.

'Well, boys,' he croaked. 'So that's it. You will both be hanged. They'll pull out your insides and poke out your eyes with red-hot irons. They'll flog you and tear off your muscles and...'

'No, sir – please – it was just a prank,' I began, but I got no further because it was then that Will Biglow turned on me. I have never felt so wretched and miserable in all my life as then, when I was about to be hanged, and my only friend in the world turned and bit the hand that had fed him all this time.

'Sir!' he cried. 'It wasn't me – it was him! It was Francis, sir! He put me up to the whole idea, sir! He said you'd be happy about it and shake our hands and it'd be a joke. We didn't know there was a real highwayman about, did we, Francis? Honest, sir – it wasn't me at all ... Francis fooled me once again, sir, just like you were always saying he did!'

'And yet there you were, Will, in disguise, with a great stick threatening to beat me round the head.'

'But not really, sir, not really!' he wept, blubbering away like a great wet cow.

I was crying myself – a few brave tears in my moment of despair. But I tried to lift up my head and confront Japes.

'Believe me, sir, it was just a trick – perhaps a misguided one, but just a trick. It's that man who is the real villain, sir!'

But Mr Japes just shook his head. 'I'm sorry, boys. I just don't believe a word of it,' he said. 'No. You are robbers on the road, and you must be hanged. It's just as well you're both tied up. I shall go and fetch the sheriff.'

He sat down on a stump and pulled his boots back on. Both of us were straining at our ropes and begging and pleading with him. Will was bellowing like a bull until the trees were shaking; but Japes just laced up his boots, shaking his head and pursing his mouth like a man who had a bad job to do.

'Enjoy the woods, boys. It may be the last spring you'll ever see.'

It was obvious to me that Japes had a heart of cold stone. Of course he didn't believe that Will and I were robbers – he was just getting his revenge for the trick we'd played on him, and for giving him such a terrible fright. I had just one card hidden up my sleeve and I was yelling to make it heard, but Will was bellowing so loudly I could hardly hear myself.

'Mr Japes, Mr Japes! Don't go to the sheriff!' I screamed. 'My uncle will make it up to you, sir, honestly he will, sir! He'll give you anything to cover this up! All your gold, sir – all your things – the horse, sir – everything … sir! He'll give you double – sir, treble! Anything, sir, any amount of money, but please don't go to the sheriff, sir, please, Mr Japes! Oh, God, Will, you stupid fart, shut up bellowing for one second…'

I thought Japes would just walk off, but finally he put his hand over Will's huge mouth so he could hear me better and I squeezed my offer out. It was enough to make greedy Japes stop and look at me. 'Well, Francis,' he said, 'If I'd wanted that money for myself I wouldn't have saved it up for my niece. But it's true that she'll be going without it because of this business. If you're hanged, that won't give me back my money…'

'Yes, sir – everything! My uncle will give it all back and more!'

'And my father, too – he'll give you a horse for

nothing – he'll pay you back! Anything on Earth!' bellowed Will, so that the woods shook and the birds flew away.

'*Silence!*' snapped Japes, just like in the classroom, and we both shut up.

He paced up and down a little, thinking. 'Well, I wonder if your guardians will be as willing as you two are to cover my costs. Still, I suppose I could pay them a visit. It may be, Francis, that your uncle will want to keep his family out of such shame – it may not. But, either way, it'll do no harm. I can always go to the sheriff afterwards, if I want. But first – your word you will not run away – not that it will do you any good, of course...'

We both swore on our lives and on the life of Jesus Christ. But, would you believe, he still wouldn't trust us? Instead, he went across the fields and found a man sowing barley and made him stand guard over us, to make sure we never escaped and that no one came along and released us, and then went off alone to fetch Will's father and my uncle. He even promised the peasant a handful of pennies to watch over us and said he expected Raymond Enterley would pay for that, too. That peasant was so delighted with his money that he spent the entire time telling us of all the dreadful things they do to highwaymen when they're caught. He even took a rabbit out of his pouch that he'd poached for his supper, and he hung it up by its neck and pulled its insides out through a hole in its stomach, to show what they would be doing to us in a few days if Mr Enterley never paid up.

Japes took hours. By the time he came back with Will's father and my uncle, I'd been weeping so much, my throat was sore for a week after.

9 ⚫ The Highwayman

I used to play in these woods when I was a child, and swim in the river – just there where the water rushes down from Fossik's Wood and takes a wide turn around the meadow. There's the deep pool we swam in, and there are the remains of the old tree whose branch we used to bounce on and jump off, feet first to make an almighty splash. Me and Tom Rolland and Ben Willoughby, we'd take the day off school on a fine summer's day for no reason at all, and Father would whip us all in a line the next day – me hardest of all, because the schoolmaster's boy should set the best example, not the worst in the whole school.

A lot has happened since then. I've fought wars and killed men and nearly died.

I stood there a while, watching the flies ripple the water and the fish rise – it was a good place to catch a fish, as well as swim – before I went on my way, up the hill again and round to the quarry where the old man waited for me. There he was, sitting on a stone in the morning mist, his horse tied by him, munching the wet grass.

'Good morning, father. And how are your aches and pains this morning?'

'Still stiff. I came off that pony like a ton of bricks. And yours? That limp is getting worse.'

'Oh, worse every day,' I said cheerfully, although it worried me. I always play fancy-free for my da, I don't know why. Because he was always trying to make me responsible, I suppose. The limp was from a wound I got in the service of the Duke, here, in the upper thigh. That's right – I'm a soldier by trade. I ran away to fight for the True Faith with Tom Howard, Duke of Norfolk. Father couldn't say no to that one, although to tell the truth I'd have run away with anyone who'd have me on at the time. We lost, we're all Protestants now. Well, God hasn't complained to me so far, so why should I bother? But the wound made me unfit to be a solider and unfit for anything else, except to beg. Or to rob.

I can't complain. I have my papers, signed by the Duke himself. I'm an upright man. I can walk into any house in the county and ask for money. Even the beggars have to give up their pennies to me. No one gives me a crust of bread or cheese – an upright man takes only money. I've earned it. It's my right, in return for my service. I can make a good living that way.

Except ... I'm a soldier. I ran away from home to fight in the wars. Don't expect a man to turn suddenly from fighter to beggar just like that. Why should I give up my calling just because I'm a little stiff? It keeps the hand in. And the money.

I sat down by my father and stretched out the stiff leg.

'Well, how did we do?'

'Very well, if you call it well,' he said. 'I got double the money from Sir Raymond, half the amount from John Biglow, a free horse and lunch whenever I need them at The White Lion.' He pulled a face – he didn't like this kind of work – and pulled a purse out of the grass and opened it up to show me. Gold and silver. A lovely sight!

'Good! And the boys?' I laughed to think of the pair of them tied up to that tree, screaming like piglets at the block! 'What a pair!'

'Both of them flogged to pieces. I doubt if they'll walk for a week. Francis is going to be sent away to join the Church, from what I gather. His uncle is a mean man, he might have given the lad more help at home rather than farming him out to me. I made him promise to pay Francis a decent keep.'

'He gave you plenty of trouble for your efforts.'

'Not a nice piece of work is Francis, I'm well rid of him. But it's Will I feel sorry for. He is a good lad, but easily used. I hope this'll teach him not to follow gaudy bright lads who promise him the world and only take away what he already has.'

'Always so keen to teach a lesson!' I said.

He smiled wryly. 'It's my job.'

'So – a good day's work then!'

'I was always too soft on you, Harry. I never flogged you hard enough when you were a lad and now here I am, helping you rob on the highway.'

'Well, you solved a few problems of your own, Da! But yes, you're a kind man to a poor thieving son,' I grinned. 'You could never have changed me, though – not a hundred schoolmasters could have. I'm just the man I am, that's all. Now then – the money! A three-way split?'

'No. I'll take my five pounds that I'd saved originally for your cousin. You and she can share the rest, two parts to her, one to you.'

'Why should I take less? I took the risk!'

'That's your job. And she's a poor woman with no husband and too many children, while you're an idle man with nothing but your pleasure to pay for. No, don't fight me, Harry, just take it, it's more than enough.'

'I wouldn't normally bother to rob someone for that little,' I grumbled. I could have held out for more, but – well, it had been such fun getting my dear old da in on a robbery, I didn't care for the money at all, hardly. Except I like money rather too much, I admit it. But there you are. Family is family.

So we embraced and kissed, and father made me promise to stay away for a few years, and we went on our separate ways, he east to Huddersfield, me off south towards Hull. I would stay away for a while, even though it wasn't strictly necessary. John Biglow may guess that I was the one who caught his son up to his tricks, but he can hardly turn me in to the sheriff. He's been telling me which of his guests to follow and rob for over a year now, and been paid well for it.

Still. I've been robbing on this stretch of road for too long. Sooner or later you get too much attention, people begin to keep an eye out for who it may be, and an upright man is a good enough suspect even when he hasn't done anything wrong.

And getting caught – it doesn't bear thinking about!

It was a grand scheme to go out on. What a bunch of fools the whole Biglow family is! I'd spotted John's stupid great son practising highway robbery a couple of weeks before bellowing, 'Your blood, your money or your life!' at the top of his great bellow, over and over again. It's a wonder half the village didn't know. I thought it was a game at first until I heard him chuckling to himself and saying how surprised Japes would be. Of course I pricked my ears up; it's my name, too. I hid in the shadows and listened, and when it became clear that he and his noble friend were planning to rob my dear old da – well. It was too good an opportunity to miss.

I was surprised Father went along with my plan – he never has before. But then this time there was so much in it for him, too. Bess got money to help with her children – he'd do anything for Bess. And he got the chance to teach a few lessons, which he can't resist. He taught two slack boys some lessons they'll never forget – Francis not to use his friends and Will not to be led by fools. He taught mean Raymond Enterley how to part with his money, and crooked John Biglow the perils of betraying his guests to the likes of me. As for me – I got a little richer – which is always welcome.

I haven't been down to Hull for three or four years now. There are plenty of ways to spend your money in a town that big. It'll last me the summer, anyhow.

I cut across the meadows. I could hear the old man singing down by the river, an old Latin hymn, and that reminded me of when I was a boy, too.

Also available in the

TUD⊕R FLASHBACKS

series from A&C Black...

BOY KING
DAVID BELBIN

Edward VI is crowned king on the death
of his father, Henry VIII – but he is only
nine years old. Power, intrigue, betrayal and
excess – can the Boy King fight his way
through the teacherous adult world?

Also available in the

TUD⊕R FLASHBACKS

series from A&C Black...

THE EYES OF DOCTOR DEE
MAGGIE PEARSON

It's 1581 and Barnabas and Temperance
make their way to London in search of
Temperance's lost love. But very quickly,
they fall into a sinister world of poltergeists,
spies, lynch mobs and even a plot to
kill Queen Elizabeth...

Also available in the

TUD⊕R FLASHBACKS

series from A&C Black...

GUNNER'S BOY
ANN TURNBULL

The Armada is coming! John's father was
killed by the Spaniards so he is desperate
to help fight the advancing Spanish fleet.
But in the end it is not revenge
he is seeking...

Another novel by this award-winning author in the

FLASHBACKS

series from A&C Black...

THE COPPER TREASURE

MELVIN BURGESS

*The ship lurched again and the deck tilted.
The copper picked up speed, slid sideways...
and crashed violently into the rail. The whole
thing hung for a moment, right on the edge
of the deck. Then it flashed red-golden light,
tipped over the edge...and dropped.*

Jamie, Ten Tons and Davies are mudlarks,
scavenging the River Thames for bits of coal,
rope and copper. When they see a huge roll of
copper fall off a ship, Ten Tons comes up
with a daring plan to retrieve it.

"A fast-paced adventure story... In (Burgess's)
hands, history comes alive."
Lindsey Fraser, The Guardian